U0100941

弦乐合奏

Lü Qiming
MONUMENTALIZE
THE MARTYRS
IN LONGHUA
STRING ENSEMBLE
(1999)

龙华祭

吕其明

总 谱

上海音乐出版社

SHANGHAI MUSIC PUBLISHING HOUSE

—— 献给

为民族解放而捐躯的烈

士们

—— To those martyrs who laid down
their lives for national liberation

弦乐合奏

Lü Qiming
MONUMENTALIZE
THE MARTYRS
IN LONGHUA
STRING ENSEMBLE
(1999)

吕其明

龙华祭

总谱

SMPH
上海音乐出版社
SHANGHAI MUSIC PUBLISHING HOUSE

龙 华 祭
MONUMENTALIZE THE MARBYRS IN LONGHUA

吕 其 明
Lü Qiming